This Little Tiger book
belongs to:

_____

_____

_____

For Jesse Edwards – in time for
the next adventure, welcome! ~ J L

LITTLE TIGER PRESS LTD,
an imprint of the Little Tiger Group
1 Coda Studios,
189 Munster Road,
London SW6 6AW
www.littletiger.co.uk

First published in Great Britain 2019
This edition published 2020
Text and illustrations copyright © Jonny Lambert 2019
Jonny Lambert has asserted his right to be identified as the author and
illustrator of this work under the Copyright, Designs and Patents Act, 1988
A CIP catalogue record for this book is available
from the British Library

LET'S ALL
CREEP
THROUGH
CROCODILE
CREEK

Jonny Lambert

LITTLE TiGER
LONDON

The sun sank slowly in the sky.

"We'd better get home before dark," said Mouse.

"Let's use the shortcut through the creek."

"Good question, Shelly," nodded Mouse,
as they all set off together.

A crocodile has a knobbly,
gnarly back.

Shelly, Rabbit and Mouse
clambered through long, thick thorns.

Ouch!

Crocodiles also have
pokey, pointy claws.

"Exactly!" laughed Mouse.
"Keep up, Rabbit!"

B-but what about the . . . ?

I don't like the sound of crocodiles at all!

Don't worry, Shelly.
You won't EVER meet a
crocodile in the creepy,
crooked creek!

On they went, swinging
through dark green vines.
"I almost forgot,"
chuckled Mouse.
"Crocs also have flippy,
whippy tails!"

Just like swingy,
springy vines?

!!!

"Urm," said Shelly as they hopped across the creek . . .

Do they also have slimy bodies like these slippy, slidey logs?

"Eek!" squeaked Shelly as they splish-splashed into a gloomy tunnel.

I'm guessing crocodiles have scary, starey eyes?

Yes, yes . . . great, googly ones to see in the dark! Come on, we're nearly home!

Pish posh! In the creepy, crooked creek? Never! Now, a **real** crocodile has a TERRIBLE, toothy mouth. And if it's open, you must never, EVER walk inside . . .

¡c!

And away they all ran from the
sneaky, snappy crocodiles.

The moon glowed brightly in the sky.
"Now how do we get home?"
huffed Shelly.

Easy peasy,
we'll take a shortcut
through the forest . . .

The fearsome,
frightful forest?
Won't there be tigers?

More hilarious adventures from Little Tiger . . .

For information regarding any of the above titles or for our catalogue, please contact us: Little Tiger Press Ltd, 1 Coda Studios, 189 Munster Road, London SW6 6AW • Tel: 020 7385 6333
E-mail: contact@littletiger.co.uk • www.littletiger.co.uk